D1682276

A giant storm swirling across Earth's surface

Planet Earth

Steve Potts

OUR SOLAR SYSTEM

A+
Smart Apple Media

☼ Published by Smart Apple Media

1980 Lookout Drive, North Mankato, MN 56003

Designed by Rita Marshall

Copyright © 2002 Smart Apple Media. International copyright reserved in all countries. No part of this book may be reproduced in any form without written permission from the publisher.

Printed in the United States of America

☼ Photographs by Photri (C. Biedel), Tom Stack & Associates (ESA, Bill & Sally Fletcher, NASA, TSADO)

☼ Library of Congress Cataloging-in-Publication Data

Potts, Steve. Planet earth / by Steve Potts. p. cm. — (Our solar system series)

Includes bibliographical references and index.

☼ ISBN 1-58340-096-6

1. Earth—Juvenile literature. [1. Earth.] I. Title.

QB631.4 .P68 2001   525—dc21   2001020122

☼ First Edition 9 8 7 6 5 4 3 2 1

Planet Earth

Earth's Atmosphere	6
Surface Temperature	12
Tectonic Plates	14
Magnetic Field	16
Additional Information	24

CONTENTS

Earth's Atmosphere

To someone from another galaxy, the third planet of our solar system, Earth, would be the most interesting. Like other planets, such as Mars and Jupiter, Earth has volcanoes, craters, wind and clouds, water and ice. But Earth is the only planet with an atmosphere of nitrogen and oxygen, making it the only known planet that can support life as we know it. ☼ Earth's atmosphere is really a collection of gases: 78 percent nitrogen, 21 percent oxygen, and 1 percent argon, with small quantities

A river canyon on Earth

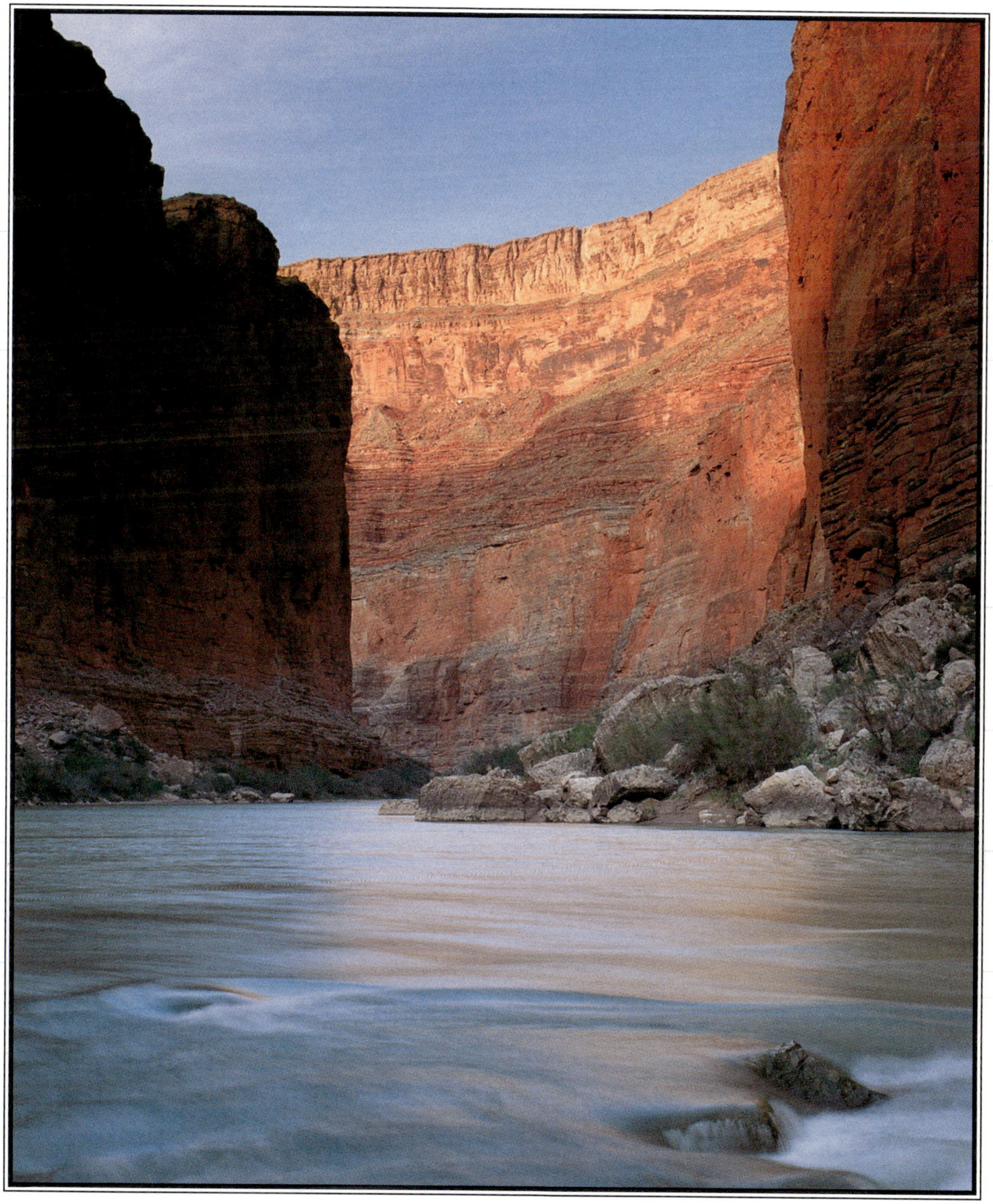

of water vapor, carbon dioxide, and other gases. The atmosphere is held in place around the planet by **gravity**.

Earth's atmosphere is made up of many layers. The two closest ones to the planet surface are the troposphere and the stratosphere. The troposphere is the bottom layer. It contains clouds and weather patterns. The stratosphere is about nine miles (14 km) above the planet's surface. It contains the ozone layer.

An Earth day is 23.93 hours, and an Earth year is 365.26 days.

The ozone layer absorbs the Sun's **ultraviolet** rays, protecting Earth's surface from damage. Recently, scientists discovered a hole in the ozone layer. It was caused by certain

chemicals that people around the world use. Many nations are

now studying ways to keep the hole from getting bigger.

Clouds form in Earth's troposphere

Large areas of water give Earth its blue color

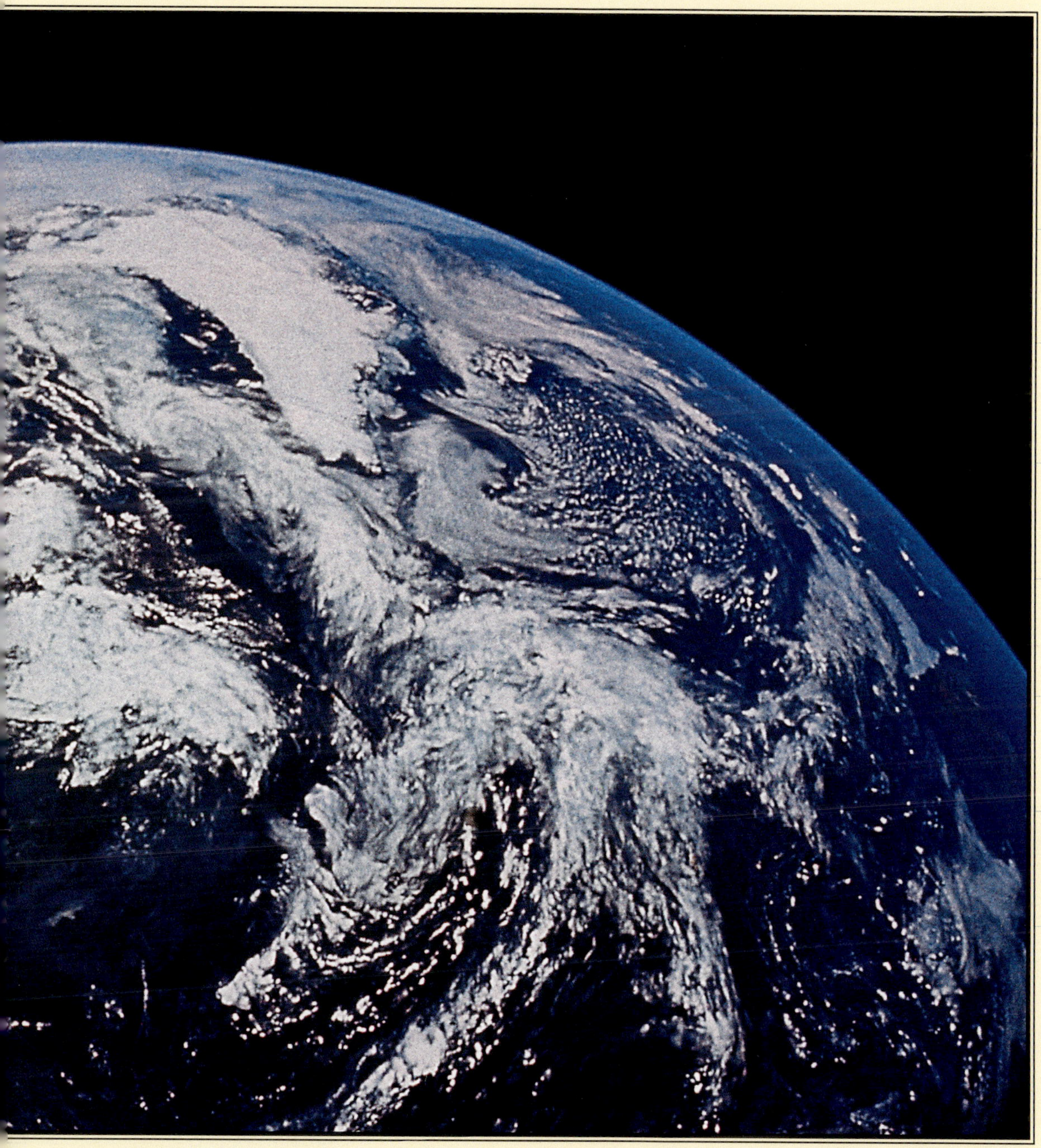

Surface Temperature

Earth's surface temperature varies widely from place to place. The lowest surface temperature ever recorded was −128.6° F (−89.2° C) in Antarctica. The highest temperature ever recorded was 136° F (57.8° C) in the Libyan desert. Some places are warm all the time, while others are cold all the time. Some places have seasonal changes: they are cold in winter and warm in summer. On average, however, Earth's surface temperature is 62° F (17° C). This is because Earth is just the

Earth's moon is about 238,900 miles (384,390 km) from Earth.

right distance from the Sun. If Earth were closer to the Sun, all

the water would boil away. If the planet were farther from the

Sun, all the water would freeze. The top layer of Earth is

Earth's distance from the Sun keeps seas from boiling

called the crust. Earth's crust began changing from the moment of the planet's birth roughly 4.5 billion years ago. Today, the planet is still changing.

Tectonic Plates

Changes occur because the crust is made up of pieces called tectonic plates. There are six major plates and many minor ones. They are always moving, floating on a layer of **molten** rock. When the plates push together or pull apart, changes in Earth's surface develop. Volcanoes may erupt. Earthquakes may occur. Mountains may grow. Islands may form. ☀ Volcanoes and earthquakes are easy to see, but the

growth of mountains takes many millions of years. Over such a

long time, the plates shift greatly. ☀ Unlike on the surface,

Shifting tectonic plates create mountains

the temperature of the planet's inner core remains very hot at all times. This core, or center, is made of solid iron and is surrounded by very hot liquid iron. On top of this liquid iron is a layer of rock.

Magnetic Field

Earth's core is like a large **magnet**. Because the core is made of molten iron that is constantly swirling around, strong electrical and magnetic currents are created. Like any magnet, Earth has two opposite magnetic poles. These are

Volcanoes spew molten rock from below Earth's crust

located near the North Pole and South Pole. The imaginary line that connects the two poles through the center of Earth is called the magnetic axis. ☀ The magnetic power that radiates from the entire planet is called the magnetic field. Travelers use Earth's magnetic field to determine the direction they are heading. The magnetized needle of a compass lines up almost parallel to Earth's magnetic field and points just slightly away from the north and south magnetic fields.

Oxygen became part of Earth's atmosphere only when green plants came into being.

Earth's magnetic currents also extend into the atmosphere and space. This area is known as the magnetosphere. When **cosmic rays** are swept toward Earth, the magnetosphere traps them. This protects Earth from high winds like those that swirl

An invisible magnetic field helps protect Earth

around Venus and Mercury. The particles are sometimes caught in one of the two radiation-filled regions circling Earth known as Van Allen belts. ☼ Although scientists have discovered much about Earth, the planet still holds many secrets. In the future, we hope to learn much more about our home—the only known planet where plant and animal life exists.

Earth's continents were once one large land area called Pangaea.

Planet Earth as seen from its moon

21

Earth is just a tiny part of the Milky Way galaxy

22

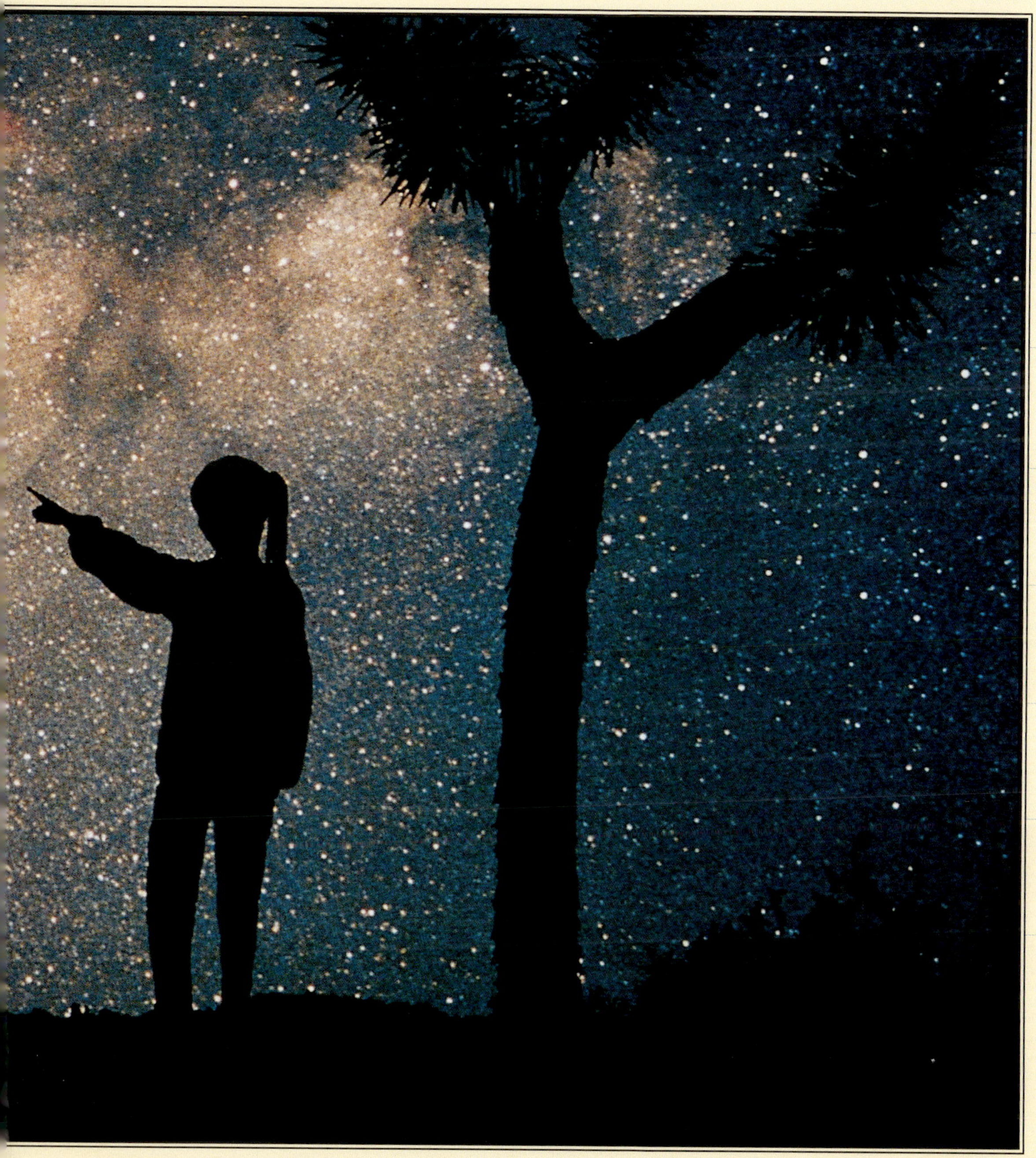

Index

atmosphere 6, 8, 18
core 16
crust 14
magnetic field 18
magnetosphere 18, 20
moon 12
ozone layer 8-9
tectonic plates 14-16
temperature 12-13, 16

Words to Know

cosmic rays—high-energy particles from the Sun and space that hit Earth's atmosphere

gravity—a force that attracts all objects in the universe; it's the force that makes things fall to the ground

magnet—a charged piece of metal; one end attracts pieces of metal and the other end pushes them away

molten—melted into liquid form

ultraviolet—a light invisible to the human eye that is emitted by the Sun

Read More

Bond, Peter. *DK Guide to Space*. New York: DK Publishing, 1999.

Couper, Heather, and Nigel Henbest. *DK Space Encyclopedia*. New York: DK Publishing, 1999.

Moignot, Daniel. *Atlas of the Earth*. New York: Scholastic, 1997.

Internet Sites

Astronomy.com
http://www.astronomy.com/home.asp

NASA: Just for Kids
http://www.nasa.gov/kids.html

Windows to the Universe
http://windows.engin.umich.edu/

The Nine Planets
http://seds.lpl.arizona.edu/nineplanets/nineplanets/

INFORMATION